THE VENUS TRAP

THE VENUS TRAP

by Evelyn E. Smith

One thing Man never counted on to take along into space with him was the Eternal Triangle—especially a true-blue triangle like this!

"What's the matter, darling?" James asked anxiously. "Don't you like the planet?"

"Oh, I love the planet," Phyllis said. "It's beautiful."

It was. The blue—really blue—grass, blue-violet shrubbery and, loveliest of all, the great golden tree with sapphire leaves and pale pink blossoms, instead of looking alien, resembled nothing so much as a fairy-tale version of Earth.

Even the fragrance that filled the atmosphere was completely delightful to Terrestrial nostrils—which was unusual, for most other planets, no matter how well adapted for colonization otherwise, tended, from the human viewpoint, anyway, to stink. Not that they were not colonized nevertheless, for the population of Earth was expanding at too great a rate to permit merely olfactory considerations to rule out an otherwise suitable planet. This particular group of settlers had been lucky, indeed, to have drawn a planet as pleasing to the nose as to the eye—and, moreover, free from hostile aborigines.

As a matter of fact, the only apparent evidence of animate life were the small, bright-hued creatures winging back and forth through the clear air, and which resembled Terrestrial birds so closely that there had seemed no point to giving them any other name. There were insects, too, although not immediately perceptible—but the ones like bees were devoid of stings and the butterflies never had to pass through the grub stage but were born in the fullness of their beauty.

However, fairest of all the creatures on the planet to James Haut—just then, anyhow—was his wife, and the expression on her face was not a lovely one.

"You do feel all right, don't you?" he asked. "The light gravity gets some people at first."

"Yes, I guess I'm all right. I'm still a little shaken, though, and you know it's not the gravity."

*

He would have liked to take her in his arms and say something comforting, reassuring, but the constraint between them had not yet been worn off. Although he had sent her an ethergram nearly every day of the voyage, the necessarily public nature of the messages had kept them from achieving communication in the deeper sense of the word.

"Well, I suppose you did have a bit of a shock," he said lamely. "Somehow, I thought I had told you in my 'grams."

"You told me plenty in the 'grams, but not quite enough, it seems."

Her words didn't seem to make sense; the strain had evidently been a little too much. "Maybe you ought to go inside and lie down for a while."

"I will, just as soon as I feel less wobbly." She brushed back the long, light brown hair which had got tumbled when she fainted. He remembered a golden rather than a reddish tinge in it, but that had been under the yellow sun of Earth; under the scarlet sun of this planet, it took on a different beauty.

"How come the preliminary team didn't include—*it* in their report?" she asked, avoiding his appreciative eye.

"They didn't know. We didn't find out ourselves until we'd sent that first message to Earth. I suppose by the time we did relay the news, you were on your way."

"Yes, that must have been it."

The preliminary exploration team had established the fact that the planet was more or less Earth-type, that its air was breathable, its temperature agreeably springlike, its mineral composition very similar to Earth's, with only slight traces of unknown elements, that there was plenty of drinkable water and no threatening life-forms. Human beings could, therefore, live on it.

It remained for the scout team to determine whether human beings would *want* to live on it—whether, in fact, they themselves would want to, because, if so, they had the option of becoming the first settlers. That was the way the system worked and, in the main, it worked well enough.

After less than two weeks, this scout team had beamed back to Earth the message that the planet was suitable for colonization, so suitable that they would like to give it the name of Elysium, if there was no objection.

There would be none, Earth had replied, so long as the pioneers bore in mind the fact that six other planets had previously been given that name, and a human colony currently existed on only one of those. No need to worry about a conflict of nomenclature, however, because the name of that other planet Elysium had subsequently been changed by unanimous vote of settlers to Hades.

*

After this somewhat sinister piece of information, Earth had added the more cheerful news that the wives and families of the scouts would soon be on their way, bringing with them the tools and implements necessary to transform the wilderness of the frontier into another Earth. In the meantime, the men were to set up the packaged buildings with which all scout ships were equipped, so that when the women came, homes would be ready for them.

THE VENUS TRAP

The men set to work and, before the month was out, they discovered that Elysium was neither a wilderness nor a frontier. It was populated by an intelligent race which had developed its culture to the limit of its physical abilities—actually well beyond the limit of what the astounded Terrestrials could have conceived its physical abilities to be—then, owing to unavoidable disaster, had started to die out.

The remaining natives were perspicacious enough to see in the Terrestrials' coming not a threat but a last hope of revivifying their own moribund species. Accordingly, the Earthmen were encouraged to go ahead building on the sites originally selected, the only ban being on the type of construction materials used—and a perfectly reasonable one under the circumstances.

James had built his cottage near the largest, handsomest tree in the area allotted to him; since there were no hostile life-forms, there was no need for a closely knit community. Everyone who had seen it agreed that his house was the most attractive one of all, for, although it was only a standard prefab, he had used taste and ingenuity to make it a little different from the other unimaginative homes.

And now Phyllis, for whom he had performed all this labor of love, for whom he had waited five long months—the tedium of which had been broken only by the intellectual pleasure of teaching English to a sympathetic native neighbor—Phyllis seemed unappreciative. She had hardly looked at the inside of the cottage, when he had shown her through, and now was staring at the outside in a blank sort of way.

The indoctrination courses had not, he reflected, reconciled her to the frontiersman's necessarily simple mode of living—which was ironic, considering that one of her original attractions for him had been her apparent suitability for the pioneer life. She was a big girl, radiantly healthy, even though a little green at the moment.

*

He just managed to keep his voice steady. "You don't like the house—is that it?

"But I *do* like it. Honestly I do." She touched his arm diffidently. "Everything would be perfect if only—"

"If only what? Is it the curtains? I'm sorry if you don't like them. I brought them all the way from Earth in case the planet turned out to be habitable. I thought blue was your favorite color."

"Oh, it is, it is! I'm mad about the curtains."

Perhaps it wasn't the house that disappointed her; perhaps it was he himself who hadn't lived up to dim memory and ardent expectation.

"If you want to know what *is* bothering me—" she glanced up apprehensively, lowering her voice as she did—"it's that tree. It's stuck on you; I just know it is."

He laughed. "Now where did you get a preposterous idea like that, Phyl? You've been on the planet exactly twenty-four hours and—"

"—and I have, in my luggage, one hundred and thirty-two ethergrams talking about practically nothing but Magnolia this, Magnolia that. Oh, I had my suspicions even before I landed, James. The only thing I didn't suspect was that she was a *tree!*"

"What are you talking about, honey? Magnolia and I—we're just friends."

"Purely a platonic relationship, I assure you," the tree herself agreed. It would have been silly for her to pretend not to have overheard, since the two were still standing almost directly underneath her. "Purely platonic."

"She's more like a sister to me," James tried to explain.

*

Phyllis stiffened. "Frankly, if I had imagined I was going to have a tree for a sister-in-law, I would have thought before I married you, James." Bursting into tears, she ran inside the cottage.

"Sorry," he said miserably to Magnolia. "It's a long trip out from Earth and an uncomfortable one. I don't suppose the other women were especially nice to her, either. Faculty wives mostly and you know how they are. . . . No, I don't suppose you would. But she shouldn't have acted that way toward you."

"Not your fault," Magnolia told him, sighing with such intensity that he could feel the humidity rise. "I know how you've been looking forward to her arrival. Rather a letdown, isn't it?"

"Oh, I'm sure it'll be all right." He tried to sound confident. "And I know you'll like Phyllis when you get to know her."

"Possibly, but so far I'm afraid I must admit—since there never has been any pretense between us—that she is a bit of a disappointment. I—and my sisters also—had expected your females, when they came, to be as upright and true blue as you. Instead, what are they? Shrubs."

The door to the cottage flew open. "A shrub, am I!" Phyllis brandished an axe which, James winced to recall, was an item of the equipment he had ordered from Earth before the scout team had learned that the trees were intelligent. "I'll shrub you!"

"Phyllis!" He wrested the axe from her grip. "That would be murder!"

"'Woodman,' as the Terrestrial poem goes," the tree remarked, "'spare that tree! Touch not a single bough! In youth it sheltered me and I'll protect it now!'"

Good of her to take the whole thing so calmly—rather, to pretend to take it so calmly, for he knew how sensitive Magnolia really was—but he was afraid this show of moral courage would not diminish Phyllis's dislike for her; those without self-control seldom appreciate those who have it.

"If you'll excuse us," he said, putting his arm around his wife's heaving shoulders, "I'd better see to Phyllis; she's a little upset. Holdover from spacesickness, I expect. Poor girl, she's a long way from home and frightened."

"I understand, Jim," Magnolia told him, "and, remember, whatever happens, you can always count on me."

*

"I must say you're not a very admirable representative of Terrestrial womanhood!" James snapped, as soon as the door had slammed behind him and his wife, leaving them alone together in the principal room of the cottage. "Insulting the very first native you meet!"

"I did not either insult her. All I said was, 'What beautiful flowers—do you suppose the fruit is edible?' How was I to know it—*she* could understand? Naturally I wouldn't dream of eating her fruit now. It would probably taste nasty anyway. And how do you think *I* felt when a *tree* answered me back? You don't care that I fainted dead away, and I've never fainted before in my life. All you care about is that old vegetable's feelings! It was bad enough, feeling for five months that someone had come between us, but to find out it wasn't some*one* but some*thing*—!"

"Phyllis," he said coldly, "I'll thank you to keep a civil tongue in your head."

Dropping into the overstuffed chair, his wife dabbed at her eyes with a handkerchief. "She wasn't so very polite to me!"

"Look, Phyllis—" he strove to make his voice calm, adult, reasonable—"you happened to have hit on rather a touchy point with her. Those trees are dioecious, you know, like us, and she isn't

11

mated. And, well, she has rather a lot of xylem zones—rings, you know."

"Are you trying to tell me she's old?"

"Well, she's no sapling any more. And, consideration aside, you know it's government's policy for us to establish good relations with any intelligent life-form we have to share a planet with. You weren't in there trying."

Phyllis put away her handkerchief with what he hoped would be a final sniff. "I suppose I shouldn't have acted that way," she conceded.

"Now you're talking like my own dear Phyllis," James said tenderly, though, as a matter of fact, he had a very remote idea of what his own dear Phyllis was like. He had met her only a couple of months before the scout mission was scheduled, and so their courtship had been brief, and the actual weeks of marriage even briefer. He had remembered Phyllis as beautiful—and she was beautiful. He had not, however, remembered her as pig-headed—and pig-headed she was, too.

"How come she hasn't a mate? I didn't think trees were choosy."

*

He wouldn't take exception to that statement, uncharitable though it was; after all, someone whose only acquaintance with trees had been with the Terrestrial variety would naturally be incapable of appreciating the total tree at its highest development.

"It's a great tragedy," he told her in a hushed tone. "There was a blight some years back and most of the male trees died off, except for a few on the other side of the planet—well out of bee-shot, even if the females there would let the females here have any pollen, which they absolutely won't."

"I don't blame them," Phyllis said coldly. Of course she would identify at once with the trees whose domestic lives seemed to be threatened.

"It's not that so much. It's that the male trees produce so little pollen."

"This would be a good place for people with hay fever then, wouldn't it?"

"And even when there is fruit, so much of it tends to be parthenocarpous—no seeds." He sighed. "The entire race is dying out."

"How is it you know so much about botany?" she asked suspiciously. "It's not your field."

"I don't know so very much, really," he smiled. "I had to learn a little, if I wanted to work the land, so I borrowed an elementary text from Cutler." Had he been a trifle idealistic in quitting his snug, if uninspiring, job on the faculty to join in this Utopian venture? So many of the other men at the university had enrolled, it had seemed a splendid idea until Phyllis's arrival.

"Daddy never had any trouble working his land and he doesn't know a thing about botany. You've been boning up on it just to please *her*!"

"Phyllis! How can you jump to conclusions without a shred of evidence?" Not that she wouldn't be able to collect such evidence later, because the allegation happened to be correct. *If, instead of coming to Elysium, I had merely gone to China, would she have thought it so odd that I studied Chinese? Then why, where the natives are trees, shouldn't I study botany? The woman is unreasonable.*

*

"And will her—people let you farm?"

THE VENUS TRAP

Now he could show her how cogently and comprehensively he could answer a logical question. "That aspect of the situation will be all right, dear, because only the trees are an intelligent species and, even of them, some aren't so bright. They won't have any more objection to our eating the other fruit and vegetables than we would have to an extraterrestrial's eating our eggs and chickens, for example. We're going to try to introduce some Earth plants here, though, as the higher forms of vegetation are dying out and we're afraid the lower might follow. Pity it's too late for a sound conservation program."

*

Phyllis said grimly, "She doesn't think it's too late for a sound conservation program. She still has hopes—far-fetched, maybe, and I'm not so sure they are. Mark my words, James, she's got designs on *you*."

"Don't be idiotic," he protested. "That would be—" he attempted to introduce a light note—"it would be miscegenation."

"These foreigners can't be expected to have our standards." And she burst into tears again. "A fine thing to go through that miserable five-month trip only to find out a tree has alienated my husband's affections."

"Oh, come on, Phyl!" He still was trying for a smile. "What would a tree see in me?"

"I'm beginning to wonder what I saw in you. You never loved me; you just wanted a wife to come out and colonize with you and b-b-breed."

What could he say? It was almost true. Phyllis was a beautiful girl and he loved her, but, if he had planned to remain as an instructor with the Romance Languages Department instead of joining the scout mission, he knew he would never have asked her to be his

14

wife . . . for her sake, of course, as well as his own. He should say something to reassure her, but the words wouldn't come.

"I don't like it here," Phyllis sobbed. "I don't like blue leaves. I don't like blue grass. I like them green, the way they're supposed to be. I hate this nasty planet. It's all wrong. I want to go home."

She was very young—less than eight years younger than he, true, but he was mature for his age. They didn't know each other very well. And, finally, there were more men than women on the planet and he had noticed that the bachelors had seemed readily disposed, upon her arrival the day before, to overlook the fact that she had no college degree. So he must be patient with her.

"There's nothing wrong about it, dear. The plants here synthesize cyanophyll instead of chlorophyll; that's why the leaves are blue instead of green. And, of course, there are different mineral constituents of the soil—more aluminum and copper, for instance, than on Earth, and some elements we haven't quite isolated yet. So, you see, they're bound to be a little different from Terrestrial trees."

"A little different I wouldn't mind," she said sulkily, "but they're a lot different without being nearly alien enough."

"Look, Phyllis—dear—those trees have been very hospitable, very kind. We owe them a lot. They themselves suggested that we come here and live with them in, so to speak, symbiosis."

"That's a fine idea!"

*

He beamed. "I knew you'd understand after I had explained it to you."

"We provide the brains and they provide the furniture."

"Phyllis! What a thing to say!"

"I've heard of man-eating trees before. I suppose there could be man-loving ones, too."

"Phyllis, these trees are as gentle and sweet as—as—" He didn't know how he could explain it to her. No one who had never been friends with a tree could appreciate the true beauty of the xylemic character. "Why, we even offered to go over to the other side of the planet and fetch some pollen for them, but they wouldn't hear of it. Unfortunately, they'd rather die than be mated to anyone they had never met."

"What a perfectly disgusting idea!"

"I don't think so. Trees can be idealistic—"

"You fetching pollen for her, I mean. Naturally she wouldn't want pollen from a tree on the other side of the planet. She wants *you!*"

"Don't be silly. Incompatibility usually exists between the pollen of one species and the stigmata of another. Besides," he added patiently, "I haven't got pollen."

"You'd better not, or it won't be her who'll have the stigmata."

"Phyllis—" he sat down on the arm of her chair and tried to embrace her—"you know that you're the only life-form I love."

"Please, James." She pushed him away. "I guess I love you, too, in spite of everything . . . but I don't want to make a public spectacle of myself."

"What do you mean now?"

"That tree would know everything that goes on. She's telepathic."

"Where did you get a ridiculous idea like that? What kind of rubbish have you been reading?"

"All right, tell me: how else did she learn to speak such good English?"

"It's because she's of a very high order of intelligence. And I suppose—" he laughed modestly—"because I'm such a good teacher."

"I don't care how good a teacher you are—a tree couldn't learn to speak a language so well in five months. She must be telepathic. It's the only explanation."

*

"Give her time," the tree advised later, as James came out on the lawn to talk to his only friend on the planet.

He hadn't seen much of the other scouts since the house-building frenzy had started, and visits among the men had decreased. The base camp, where the bachelors and the older married couples lived, was located a good distance away from his land, for he had raised his honeymoon cottage far from the rest; he had wanted to have his Phyllis all to himself. In the idyll he had visualized for the two of them, she would need no company but his. Little had he imagined that, within twenty-four hours of her arrival, he would be looking for company himself.

"I suppose so," he said, kicking at a root. "Oh, I'm sorry, Maggie; I didn't think."

"That's all right," Magnolia said bravely. "It didn't really hurt. That female has got you all upset, you poor boy."

James muttered a feeble defense of his wife.

"Jim, forgive me if I speak frankly," the tree went on in a low rustle, "but do you think she's really worthy of you?"

"Of course she is!"

"Surely on your planet you could have found a mate more admirable, high-minded, exemplary—more, in short, like yourself. Or are all the human females inferior specimens like Phyllis?"

"They're—she suits me," James said doggedly.

"Of course, of course. It's very noble of you to defend her; you would have disappointed me if you had said anything else, and I honor you for it, James."

He kicked at one of the pebbles. The tree meant well, he knew, yet, like so many well-meaning friends, she succeeded only in dispiriting him. It was almost like being back at the faculty club.

"I don't suppose a clod like her would have brought any more books along," the tree changed the subject. James's own library had been insufficient to slake the tree's intellectual thirst, so he had gone all over the planet to borrow books for Magnolia. Dr. Lakin, at Base, who had formerly taught English literature, possessed a fine collection which he had been reluctant to lend until he had learned that they were not for James but for a tree. At that, he had fetched the books himself, since he was anxious to meet her.

"A lot of the trees here have learned the English language," he had told James, "but none seems to have developed a taste for its literature. Your Magnolia is undoubtedly a superior specimen. Excellent natural taste, too—perhaps a little unformed when it comes to poetry and the more sophisticated aspects of life, but she'll learn, she'll learn."

*

Unfortunately, the same, James knew, could hardly be said of his wife. "Phyllis did bring some books," he told Magnolia.

"For you, no doubt. That was kind of her. I'm sure she has many good qualities which will unfold one by one, as her meristems start differentiating. I hope you don't feel I've been too—well, personal, Jim. I was only trying to help. If I've gone too far. . . . "

"Of course not, Maggie. After all—" he laughed bitterly—"I do know you better than I know her."

"We *have* been good friends, haven't we, Jim? It was rather nice—these five months we spent alone together. For the first time in my life, I have never regretted being so far from my sisters. 'And this

18

our life, exempt from public haunt, finds tongues in trees, books in the running brooks, sermons in stones, and good in everything.'"

Her blue leaves shone violet in the scarlet rays of the setting sun; the gold of her trunk was lit with red radiance. She was the most beautiful creature he had ever seen . . . but she was a tree, not a woman.

"I'm sure she'll fit in after a while," Magnolia continued. "Perhaps she isn't well. She seems to guttate an awful lot. Do you suppose she's been overwatered?"

"That wasn't guttation," James said heavily. "It was tears. It means she's unhappy."

"Unhappy? Perhaps she won't fit in on this planet, in which case she should by all means go back to Earth. It's cruel and unfair to keep an intelligent—loosely speaking—life-form anywhere against her will, don't you think?"

"She'll be happy here," James vowed. "I'll *make* her happy."

"Well, I certainly hope you can manage it! By the way, do you suppose you'll have a chance to read me the books she brought, or will she be keeping you too busy?"

"I'll never be too busy to read to you, Magnolia."

"That's very nitrogenous of you, Jim. Our—intellectual communions have meant a lot to me. I'd hate to have to give them up."

"So would I," he said. "But there won't be any need to. Phyllis will understand."

"I certainly hope so. I so admire your English literature. It's so deeply cognizant of the really meaningful things in life. And if your coming to this planet has served only to add poetry to our cultural heritage, it would be reason enough to welcome you with open limbs. For it was a truly perceptive versifier who wrote the immortally simple lines: 'Poems are made by fools like me, but only God can make a tree.'

"And such a charming tune to go with it, too," Magnolia went on. "We have always sung the music that the wind and the rain have taught us, but, until you came, we never thought of putting words and melody together to form one glorious whole. 'A tree that may in summer wear,'" she caroled in a pleasing contralto, "'a nest of robins in her hair.' By the way, Jim, ever since reading that poem, I've been meaning to ask you precisely what are robins and do you think they'd look well in my hair, by which, I suppose the bard refers, in a somewhat pedestrian flight of fancy, to leaves?"

"They're a kind of bird," he said drearily.

"Birds—nesting in my hair! I wouldn't think of allowing it. But then I suppose Terrestrial birds are quite different from ours? More housebroken, shall we say?"

"Everything's different," James said and, for an irrational moment, he hated everything that was blue that should have been green, everything sweet that should have been vicious, everything intelligent that should have been mindless.

*

Since matters could not grow much worse, they improved to a degree. After a day or two had passed, Phyllis, being a conscientious girl, came to realize how wrong it had been for her as a Terrestrial immigrant to show overt hostility toward a native of the planet that had welcomed her.

"But how can she be a—a person?" Phyllis wanted to know, when they were inside the cottage, for she had learned to hold her tongue when they were near Magnolia or any of her sisters, who, though they could not speak the language as fluently as she, understood it very well and eavesdropped at every possible opportunity in order, they said, to improve their accents. "She's a tree. A plant. And plants are just vegetables." She stabbed her needle energetically through the tablecloth she was embroidering.

"You mustn't project Terrestrial attitudes upon Elysian ones," James said, patiently looking up from his book. "And don't underestimate Magnolia's capabilities. She has sense organs, and motor organs, too. She can't move from where she is, because she's rooted to the ground, but she's capable of turgor movements, like certain Terrestrial forms of vegetation—for example, the sensitive plant or blue grass."

"Blue grass," Phyllis exclaimed. "I'm sick of blue grass. I want green grass."

"However, these trees have conscious control of their *pulvini*, whereas the Earth's plants don't, and so they can do a lot of things that Earth plants can't."

"It sounds like a dirty word to me."

"*Pulvini* merely means motor organs."

"Oh."

*

He closed his book, which was a more advanced botany text, covered with the jacket of a French novel in order to spare Phyllis's feelings. "Darling, can't you get it through your pretty head that they're intelligent life-forms? If it'll make it easier for you to think of them as human beings who happen to look like trees, then do that."

"That's exactly what I *am* doing. And I'm quite sure she thinks of you as a tree who happens to look like a human being."

"Phyllis, sometimes I think you're being deliberately difficult. Do you know one of the reasons why I took such pains to teach Magnolia English? It was that I hoped she would be a companion for you, that you could talk to each other when I had to be away from home."

THE VENUS TRAP

"Why do you call her Magnolia? She isn't a lot like one."

"Isn't she? I thought she was. You see, I don't know so much botany, after all." Actually, he had picked that name for the tree because it expressed both the arboreal and the feminine at the same time—and also because it was one of the loveliest names he knew. But he couldn't tell Phyllis that; there would be further misunderstanding. "Of course she has a name in her own language, but I can't pronounce it."

"They *do* have a language of their own then?"

"Naturally, though they don't get much chance to speak it, since they've grown so few and far apart that verbal communication has become difficult. They communicate by a network of roots that they've developed."

"I don't think that's so clever."

"I merely said . . . oh, what's the use of trying to explain everything to you? You just don't want to understand."

*

Phyllis put down her needlework and closed her eyes. "James," she said, opening them again, "it's no use pretending. I've been trying to be sympathetic and understanding, but I can't do it. That tree—I've forced myself to be nice to her, but the more I see of her, the more convinced I am that she's trying to steal you from me."

Phyllis was beginning to poison his mind, he thought, because it had seemed to him also, in his last conversation with Magnolia, that he had discerned more than ordinary warmth in her attitude toward him . . . and perhaps a trace of spite toward his wife?

Preposterous! The tree had only been trying to cheer him up as any friend might reasonably do. After all, a tree and a man. . . . Nonsense! One had an anabolic metabolism, one a catabolic.

But this was a different kind of tree. She spoke, she read, she was capable of conscious turgor movements. And he, he had often thought secretly, was a different kind of man. Whereas Phyllis. . . .

But that was disloyalty—to the type as well as the individual. The tree could be a companion to him, but she could not give him sons to work his land; she could not give him daughters to populate his planet; moreover, she did not, could not possibly know what human love meant, while Phyllis could at least learn.

"Look, dear," he said, sitting down beside his wife on the couch and taking her hand in his. She didn't draw away this time. "Suppose that what you say is true—not that it is, of course. Just because the tree has a crush on me doesn't mean I necessarily have a crush on her, does it?"

His wife looked up at him, her rose-red lips parted, her moss-gray eyes shining. "Oh, if only I could believe that, James!"

"Anyhow, she doesn't know what the whole thing's about, poor kid!"

"Poor *kid!*"

"Phyllis, you know you're prettier than any tree." That was not literally true, but reason was useless; he had to make his point in terms she could understand. "And, remember, she's got a lot of rings—she must be centuries old—while you are only nineteen."

"Twenty," Phyllis corrected. "I had a birthday on the ship."

"Well, you certainly must allow me to wish you a happy birthday, darling."

She was in his arms at last; he was about to kiss her, and the tree seemed very remote, when she drew back. "But are you sure she doesn't—she isn't—she can't be watching us?"

"Darling, I swear it!" "*Lady, by yonder blessed moon I swear, that tips with silver all these fruit-tree tops*". . . . But he had sense enough not to say it, and Elysium had not one blessed moon, but three, and everything was all right.

For a while anyway.

*

"I see your wife is developing a corm," the tree remarked, as James paused for a chat. He hadn't much time to be sociable those days, for there was such a lot of work to be done, so many preparations to be made, so many things to be requisitioned from Earth. The supply ships were beginning to come now, bringing necessities and an occasional luxury for those who could afford it.

"She's pregnant," James explained. "Happened before I left Earth."

"How do you mean?"

"She's about to fruit. Didn't I read that zoology book to you?"

"Yes, but—oh, James, it all seems so vulgar! To fruit without ever having bloomed—how squalid!"

"It all depends on how you look at it," he said. "I—that is, we had hoped that when the baby came, you would be godmother to it. You know what that is, don't you?"

"Of course I do. You read *Cinderella* to me. I know it's a great honor. But I'm afraid I must decline."

"Why? I thought you were my—our friend."

"Jim, there is something I must confess: my feelings toward you are not merely those of a friend. Although Phyllis doesn't have too many rings of intellect, she is a female, so she knew all along." Magnolia's leaves rustled diffidently. "I feel toward you the way I never felt toward any intelligent life-form, but only toward the sun, the soil, the rain. I sense a tropism that seems to incline me toward you. In fact, I'm afraid, Jim, in your own terms, I love you."

"But you're a tree! You can't love me in my own terms, because trees can't love in the way people can, and, of course, people can't

24

love like trees. We belong to two entirely different species, Maggie. You can't have listened to that zoology book very attentively."

"Our race is a singularly adaptable one or we wouldn't have survived so long, Jim, or gone so far in our particular direction. It's lack of fertility, not lack of enterprise, that's responsible for our decline. And I think your species must be an adaptable one, too; you just haven't really tried. Oh, James, let us reverse the classical roles—let me be the Apollo to your Daphne! Don't let Phyllis stand in our way. The Greek gods never let a little thing like marriage interfere with their plans."

*

"But I love Phyllis," he said in confusion. "I love you, too," he added, "but in a different way."

"Yes, I know. More like a sister. However, I have plenty of sisters and I don't need a brother."

"We're starting a conservation program," he tried to comfort her. "We have every hope of getting some pollen from the other side of the planet once we have explained to the trees there how far we can make a little go, and you've got to accept it; you mustn't be silly about it."

"It isn't the same thing, Jim, and you know it. One of the penalties of intelligence is a diffusiveness of the natural instincts. I would rather not fruit at all than—"

"Magnolia, you just don't understand. No matter how much you—well, pursue me, I can never turn into a laurel tree."

"I didn't—"

"Or any kind of tree! Look, some more books were just sent over from Base."

Magnolia gave a rueful rustle. "Just were sent? Didn't they come over a month ago?"

James flushed. "I know I haven't had a chance to do much reading to you in the last few weeks, Maggie—or any at all, in fact—but I've been so busy. After the baby's born, things will be much less hectic and we'll be able to catch up."

"Of course, James. I understand. Naturally your family comes first."

"One of the books that came was an advanced zoology text that might make things a little clearer."

"I should very much like to hear it. When you have the time to spare, that is."

"Tell you what," he said. "I'll get the book and read you the chapter on the reproductive system in mammals. Won't take more than an hour or so."

"If you're in a hurry, it can wait."

"No," he told her. "This will make me feel a little less guilty about having neglected you."

*

"Whereupon the umbilical cord is severed," he concluded, "and the human infant is ready to take its place in the world as a separate entity. Now do you understand, Magnolia?"

"No," she said. "Where do the bees come in?"

"I thought you were in such a hurry to get to Base, James," Phyllis remarked sweetly from the doorway, wiping her reddening hands on a dish towel.

"I am, dear." He slipped the book behind his back; it was possible that, in her present state of mind—induced, of course, by her delicate condition—Phyllis might misunderstand his motive in reading that particular chapter of that particular book to that particular tree. "I just stopped for a chat with Magnolia. She's agreed to be godmother to the baby."

"How very nice of her. Earth Government will be so pleased at such a *fine* example of rapport with the natives. You might even get a medal. Wouldn't that be nice? . . . James," she hurried on, before he could speak, "you still haven't found any green-leafed plants on the planet, have you? Have you looked everywhere? Have you looked *hard?*"

"Haven't I told you time and time again, Mrs. Haut," the tree said, "that there aren't any—that there can't be any? It's impossible to synthesize chlorophyll from the light rays given off by our sun—only cyanophyll. What do you want with a green-leafed plant, anyway?"

Phyllis's voice broke. "I think I'd lose my mind if I was convinced that I'd never see a green leaf again. All this awful blue, blue, blue, all the time, and the leaves never fall, or, if they do, there are new ones right away to take their place. They're always there—always blue."

"We're everblue," Magnolia explained. "Sorry, but that's the way it is."

"Jim, I hate to hurt your feelings, but I just have to take down those curtains. The colors—I can't stand it!"

*

"Pregnant women sometimes get fanciful notions," James said to the tree. "It's part of the pregnancy syndrome. Try not to pay any attention."

"Kindly don't explain me to a tree!" Phyllis cried. "I have a right to prefer green, don't I?"

"There is, as your proverb says, no accounting for strange tastes," the tree murmured. "However—"

"We're going to have a formal christening," James interrupted, for the sake of the peace. "We thought we should, since ours will be the first baby born on the planet. Everybody on Elysium will come—that is, all the human beings. Only because they *can* come, you know;

we'd love to have the trees if they were capable of locomotor movement. You'll get to widen your social contacts, Maggie. Dr. Lakin and Dr. Cutler will probably be here; I know you'll be glad to see Dr. Lakin again, and you've been anxious to meet Dr. Cutler. They've been asking after you, too. I think Dr. Lakin is planning to write a monograph on you for the *Journal of the American Association of Professors of English Literature*—with your permission, of course."

"Christening—that's one of your native festivals, isn't it? It should be most interesting."

"That's right," Phyllis murmured. "It will be Christmas soon. I'd almost forgotten. It'll be the first Christmas I've ever spent away from home. And there won't be any snow or—or anything." She started to guttate—to cry again.

"Cheer up, honey," Jim said. "It won't be as bad as you think, because I didn't forget Christmas was coming. There's something specially nice for you on its way from Earth; I only hope it gets here on time." Phyllis sniffled. "Maybe we'll have a Christmas party, too. Would you like that?" But she remained unresponsive.

He turned to the tree. "Christening's entirely different, though," he explained. "It's—I guess naming the fruit would be the best way to describe it."

"Is that so?" Magnolia said. "What kind of fruit do you expect to have, Mrs. Haut? Oranges? Bananas? As your good St. Luke says, the tree is known by its fruit. You look as if yours might be a watermelon."

"Why, the—idea!" Phyllis choked. "Are you going to stand there, James, and let that *vegetable* insult me?"

"I'm sure she didn't mean to," he protested. "She got confused by—that zoology book I read her."

The door slammed behind his weeping wife.

"I don't think you quite understand, Maggie," he said. "In fact, sometimes I almost think you, too, don't want to understand."

"I know what kind of fruit it's going to be," the tree concluded triumphantly. "Sour apples."

*

"Ouch," exclaimed Magnolia, "that tickles! There's more to acting as a Christmas tree than I had anticipated from your glowing descriptions, Jim."

"Here, dear," Phyllis said, "maybe you'd better let me put the decorations on her."

"You can't get on the ladder in your condition," he said, apprehensive not only for her welfare but for the tree's. Phyllis had not taken kindly to the idea of having Magnolia as official Christmas tree, suggesting that, if she must participate in the ceremonies, it might be better in the capacity of Yule log. However, Jim knew Magnolia would be offended if any other tree were chosen to be decorated.

"I'll manage all right," he assured his wife. "If you want to be useful, you might put on some coffee and make sandwiches or something. The bachelors are coming over from Base with that equipment that arrived yesterday, and they'll probably be glad of a snack before turning in."

"The coffee's already on and the canapes made," Phyllis smiled. "And I've baked cookies, too, and whipped up a batch of penuche. What kind of a Christmas party do you think it would be without refreshments?"

"Very efficient, isn't she?" Magnolia remarked, as the battery-powered lights that James had affixed to her began to wink on, for the deep red-violet dusk had already fallen and the first moon was rising. "Have you thought, Mrs. Haut, that if you fruit today, it will save the expense of another festival?"

"I don't expect to fruit for another two months," Phyllis said coldly, "and why shouldn't we have another festival? We can afford it and I like parties. I haven't been to one since the day I landed."

"Is the life out here getting a little quiet for you, petiole?" the tree asked solicitously. "It must be hard when one has no intellectual resources upon which to draw."

*

Phyllis held her peace for ten seconds; then, "I wonder where those boys can be," she said. "I hope they bring some pickles along. I asked to have some sent, but I'm accustomed to having no attention paid to what I want."

"There's a surprise coming for you, Phyllis," James could not help telling her again, hoping to arouse some semblance of interest. "Something I know you'll love. . . . And for you, too," he said courteously to Magnolia.

"You mean the same surprise for both, or a surprise apiece?" the tree asked.

"Oh, one for each, of course."

"I see the lights of the 'copter now!" Phyllis cried and, running out into the middle of the lawn, began waving her handkerchief. He hadn't seen her so pleasantly excited for a long time.

"I don't suppose I'll need to turn on the landing lights," he said to Magnolia. "You should do the trick."

"Am I all finished?" she rustled anxiously. "I do wish I could see myself. How do I look?"

"Splendid. I've never had as beautiful a Christmas tree as you, Maggie," he told her with complete honesty. "Not even on Earth."

"I'm glad, Jim, but I still wish I could be more to you than just a Christmas tree."

"Shh. The others might hear."

For the helicopter had landed and the visitors were pouring out, with shouts of admiration. Not only the bachelors had come—and in full force—but some of the older men from Base, who apparently felt they could manage to do without their wives for twelve hours, even if those hours included Christmas Eve. He wondered where he and Phyllis could put them all, but some could sleep outside, if need be, for it was never cold on Elysium. The winds were gentle and the rains light and fragrant.

*

While the visitors were crowding around Phyllis and the tree, James rooted eagerly through the packages they had brought, until he found what he wanted. Then he rushed over to the group. "I know I should wait until tomorrow, but I want to give the girls their presents now." The other men smiled sympathetically, almost as joyful as he. "Merry Christmas, Magnolia!" He hoped Phyllis would understand that it was etiquette which dictated that the alien life-form should get her gift first.

"Thank you," the tree said. "I am deeply touched. I don't believe anyone ever gave me a present before. What is it?"

"Liquid plant food—vitamins and minerals, you know. For you to drink."

"What fun!" she exclaimed in pretty excitement. "Pour some over me right now!"

"Not so fast, Jim, boy!" Dr. Cutler, the biologist, snatched the jug from James' hand. "First you-all better let me take a sample of this here stuff back to Base to test on a lower life-form, so's I can make sure it won't do anything bad to Miss Magnolia. Might have iron in it and I have a theory that iron may not be beneficial for the local vegetation."

"Oh, thank you!" the tree rustled. "It's so very thoughtful of you, Doctor, but I'm sure Jim would never give me anything that would injure me."

"I'm sure he isn't fixing to do a thing like that, ma'am, but he's no botanist."

"And for you, Phyllis. . . . " James handed his wife the awkward bundle to unwrap for herself.

She tore the papers off slowly. "Oh, Jim, darling, it's—it's—"

"You wanted a bit of green, so I ordered a plant from Earth. You like it? I hope you do."

"Oh, *Jim!*" She embraced him and the pot simultaneously. "More than *anything!*"

"It won't stay green," Magnolia observed. "Either it'll turn blue or it'll die. Puny-looking specimen, isn't it?"

"Well," said James, "it's only a youngster. I guess this Christmas is too early, but next Christmas there ought to be berries. It's a holly plant, Phyl."

"Holly," she repeated, her voice shaking a little. "*Holly.*" She and Dr. Cutler exchanged glances.

"I told you, Miz Phyllis, ma'am—he may know the first thing about botany, but he doesn't know anything after that."

"Jim," Phyllis said, linking her free arm through his, "I misjudged you. Dr. Cutler is right. You don't know so very much about botany, after all."

*

He looked at her blankly. Her voice was trembling, and not with tears this time. "I love this little plant; it's just what I wanted . . . but there aren't ever going to be any berries, because, to have berries, you have to have two plants. And the right two. Holly's di—dio—it's just like us."

"Oh," James said, feeling thoroughly inadequate. "I'm sorry."

"But you mustn't be sorry. I'm going to plant it here on Elysium, and I hope it will stay green in spite of what she says, and it'll have blossoms anyway . . . and it was very, very sweet of you, dear."

She kissed his cheek.

"Is this one a boy or a girl?" Magnolia asked.

"You-all can't tell till it blooms, Miss Magnolia, ma'am," Dr. Cutler informed her.

"Maybe I can. Hand it up here, please."

Phyllis paused for an irresolute moment, then, smiling nervously at her guests, obliged.

"It's a boy," Magnolia announced, after a minute. "A boy." She gave back the pot reluctantly. "Phyllis," she said, "you and I have never been friends and I admit that it's been my fault just as much as yours."

"As much as mine?" Phyllis echoed. "I like that—" and was going to go on when she obviously recollected that they had company, and stopped.

"So I know it's presumptuous of me to ask you a favor."

"Yes, Magnolia?" Phyllis said, her fine cornsilk eyebrows arched a trifle. "What is this favor?"

"When you plant the little fellow—you said you were going to, anyhow—would you plant him near me?"

Phyllis looked down at the plant she held cradled in her arms and then up at the tree. "Of course, Magnolia," she said, frowning slightly. "I didn't realize. . . . " Her voice began to tremble.

"I *have* been pretty rotten, haven't I?" She looked toward James, but he turned his glance away.

"Just because you were a plant," Phyllis continued, "didn't mean I had to be a b-b-beast. It must have been awful for you, seeing me like this, practically crowing over you, and knowing that you yourself would never have the chance to be a m-m-m-mother."

"'Full many a flower is born to blush unseen,'" Magnolia said sadly, "'and waste its sweetness on the desert air.'"

*

Phyllis was crying unashamedly now. "I'll plant him right next to you—Maggie. I want you to have him. He can be your baby."

"Thank you, Phyl," Maggie said softly. "That's very . . . blue of you."

"Although I think that's a jim-dandy idea," the biologist said, "and I sure wouldn't want to do anything to discourage it, being real interested in the results of an experiment like that my own self, I don't think you ought to feel so mean about it, Miz Phyllis. If all she wanted—begging your pardon, Miss Magnolia, ma'am—was a baby, why didn't she take an interest in the holly until she found out it was a male? Why wouldn't a little old girl holly have done as well?"

"Why—why, you scheming vegetable!" Phyllis exploded at Magnolia, clutching the holly plant to her protective bosom. "He's much too young for you, and I'm going to plant him far away, where he can't possibly fall into your clutches."

"Now, Miss Phyllis, we-all mustn't look at things out of their proper perspective."

"Then why did you take your hat off when you were introduced to Miss Magnolia, Cutler?" Dr. Lakin asked interestedly.

"Sir, where I come from, we respect femininity, whether it be animal, vegetable or mineral. Nonetheless, we-all got to remember, though Miss Magnolia is unquestionably a lady, she is not a woman."

Phyllis began to laugh hysterically. "You're right!" she gasped. "I had almost forgotten *she* was only a tree. And that *it* is only a little Christmas holly plant that's probably going to die, anyway—they almost always do."

"That's cruel, Phyllis," James said, "and you know it is."

"Do you really think I'm cruel? Are you going to tell the Society for the Prevention of Cruelty to Vegetables on me? But why am I cruel? I'm giving her the holly. That's what she wants, isn't it? Do you hear that, Miss Magnolia, ma'am? *He's* all yours. We'll plant *him* next to you—right away. And I hope *he* doesn't die. I hope *he* grows up to make you a good husband."

*

"She's really quite remarkable," Dr. Lakin said to James later that same evening, after the planting ceremonies were over and the rest of the party had gone into the cottage for fresh coffee and more sandwiches and cookies and penuche. "Quite remarkable. You're a lucky man, Haut."

"Thank you, sir," James replied abstractedly. "I'm sure Phyllis will be pleased to—"

"*Phyllis!* Oh, Mrs. Haut is a very remarkable woman, of course. A handsome, strong girl; she'll make a splendid mother, I'm sure. But I was referring to Miss Magnolia. She's a credit to you, my boy. If for no other reason, your name will go down in the history of our colony as that of the guide and mentor of Miss Magnolia. That's quite a tree you have there."

James looked at the dark form of the tree—for the lights had been turned out—silhouetted against the three pale moons and the violet night. "Yes, she is," he said.

"You're fortunate to be her neighbor . . . and her friend."

"Yes, I am."

35

"Well, I expect I'd better join the rest. Are you coming on in, Jim?"

"In a little while, sir. I thought I'd—I wanted to have a word with Magnolia. I won't be long."

"Of course, of course. I'm delighted to see that there is such an excellent relationship between you. . . . Good night, Miss Magnolia!" he called.

"Good night, Dr. Lakin," the tree replied, politely enough, but it was obvious that she was preoccupied with her new charge, who stood as close to her as it was possible to plant him and yet allow room for him to grow.

*

The door closed. James walked across the lawn until he was quite near Magnolia. "Maggie," he whispered, reaching out to touch her trunk—smooth it was, and hard, but he could feel the vibrant life pulsing inside it. Certainly she was not a plant, not *just* a plant, even though she was a tree. She was a native of Elysium, neither animal nor vegetable, unique unto the planet, unique unto herself. "Maggie."

"Yes, Jim. Don't you think his silhouette is so graceful there in the moonlight? He isn't really puny—just frail."

"Maggie, you're not serious about this holly?"

"What do you mean?" And still he didn't have her full attention. Would he ever have it again?

"Serious about raising him to be your—your—"

"Why not, Jim?"

"It's impossible."

"Is it? It certainly is far more possible with him, isn't it? That much I understood from your zoology books."

"I suppose so."

"Besides, I have nothing to lose, have I?"

36

"But even if it were possible, wouldn't it be humiliating for you? The creature's mindless!"

Magnolia's leaves rustled in the darkness. She was laughing—a little bitterly. "Your Phyllis isn't your intellectual equal, Jim, and yet you say you love her and I suppose you do. Am I not entitled to my follies also?"

But she couldn't compare Phyllis to a holly plant! It was unreasonable.

"He may die, of course," Magnolia said. "I've got to be prepared for that. The soil is different, the air is different, the sun is different. But the chances are, if he survives, he'll turn blue. And if he turns blue, who knows what other changes might be brought about? Maybe the plants on your Earth aren't inherently mindless, Jim. Maybe they just didn't have a chance. 'Know ye the land where the cypress and myrtle are emblems of deeds that are done in their clime. . . ?' That land isn't Earth, Jim, so it might just possibly be Elysium."

*

Again he didn't say anything. What he wanted to say, he had no right to say, so he kept silent.

"It'll be a chance for me, too, Jim. At least we're both plants, he and I. That gives us a headstart."

"Yes, I suppose it does."

"Intellect doesn't count for much in the propagation of the species. Life goes on without regard for reason, and that's mainly what we're here for, to make sure that life goes on—if we're here for anything at all. Thanks to your kind, Jim, life will continue on this planet; it will certainly be your kind of life—and I hope it can be ours as well."

"Yes," he said. "I hope so, too."

And he did, but he wished it didn't have to continue in quite that way. Perhaps it was a trick of the three moons, but the holly plant's leaves seemed to have changed color. They were no longer green, but almost blue—powder blue.

"You'd best be getting on to your party, Jim," Magnolia said. "You wouldn't want to be remiss in your duties as host. And please close the door gently when you go inside. The little holly plant's asleep."

As he closed the door carefully behind him, he heard a burst of laughter coming from the kitchen, where the guests apparently had assembled—raucous animal laughter—and, rising shrill and noisy above it, Phyllis's company laugh.